j
S

6519

Snavely, Ellen
Shoes for Angela

Shoes for Angela

by *Ellen Snavely*

ILLUSTRATED BY LEONARD SHORTALL

Follett Publishing Company

Chicago • New York

LIBRARY OF CONGRESS CATALOG CARD NUMBER: 62-15672

Angela liked shoes.

But Angela had only two pairs.

One pair was brown, for school.

One pair was black, for good.

Angela said,

"Mother, I need more shoes.

I really do."

"Your feet are still growing,"
her mother said.

"Two pairs of shoes are enough."

Angela got an idea.

She wrote to her grandmother.

"Dear Grandmother,

You asked what I want for my birthday.
I would only like shoes, and my size is 2.

Please tell all the aunts and uncles and
cousins. I can use most any kind.

Love,

Angela"

Now Angela had many aunts and many, many uncles. She had dozens of cousins both big and small.

When they got the news, the aunts all ran out to buy shoes for Angela.

"She is so sensible," they all said.

And the uncles ran out to buy shoes for Angela.

"What a fine little girl," they all said.

All the cousins who had any money ran
out and got shoes for Angela.

And of course Grandmother got shoes.

On Angela's birthday, the mail truck
stopped at her house.

The mailman came up the walk with a
pile of boxes higher than his head.

Angela opened the boxes.

Then she laughed and laughed and laughed.

For in each box there was a pair of shoes.

There were white shoes,

      red shoes,

      green shoes,

      black shoes,

      pink shoes,

      and blue shoes!

Now Angela had red shoes to wear
with her red skirt.

She had green shoes to wear with her
green skirt.

She had shoes with straps and shoes
without straps.

She had pink shoes to wear for dancing.

She had black boots to wear when
she rode her pony.

She had shiny black shoes to wear
to church.

She had high red boots to wear in the
snow and short yellow boots to wear
in the rain.

And one young uncle sent her a pair of
green flippers to wear in the pool!

All of the shoes were just the right
size. Size 2.

Now Angela had shoes in every pocket in her shoe bag.

She had shoes under her bed and under her dresser.

She had shoes on her closet shelf and shoes on her closet floor.

Now Angela had so many shoes that she got quite careless.

Once she walked right out of a pair in the living room.

And sometimes she left a pair in the kitchen or on the steps.

Once she forgot and left her blue shoes
in the yard.

Rain fell in the night. In the morning
the blue shoes were full of water.

Angela's room looked terrible.

Mother said,

"Oh, Angela! There are shoes here,
shoes there, shoes, shoes, everywhere!

And all you need is just two pairs."

The shoes were fun, and Angela liked them.

But they were a lot of work!

Sometimes Angela had to change her play shoes

for her dancing shoes

and her dancing shoes

for her riding boots

and her riding boots

for her shoes for church.

All the shoes had to be cleaned.

All the shoes had to be shined.

Angela's room was a terrible mess of
nothing but SHOES.

One morning Angela put on the blue
shoes.

"Ouch!" said Angela.

They hurt.

She put on the red shoes.

"Ouch, ouch!" said Angela.

They hurt too.

She put on the pink shoes for dancing.

"Ouch, ouch, ouch!"

Mother said,

"I'm afraid these shoes are all too small."

Mother looked to see if Angela was going to cry.

But she wasn't.

"I guess we'll just have to go to the shoe store today," said Mother.

At the shoe store they bought a pair of
brown shoes, size 3, for school.

And they bought a pair of black shoes,
size 3, for good.

Angela wore the new brown shoes home.

Angela said, "What will we do with all my size 2 shoes?"

Mother said, "The PTA is having a sale. We'll take the shoes there."

And they did.

A little girl with yellow hair got the red shoes.

A little girl with brown hair got the pink shoes.

A little girl with blue eyes got the blue shoes.

All Angela's shoes were on size 2 feet, and everybody was happy.

Now in Angela's closet there are two
pairs of shoes.

Brown ones for school and black ones
for good.

And Angela says, "Next birthday,
I think I'll ask for hats."

SHOES FOR ANGELA

Reading Level: Level Two. *Shoes for Angela* has a total vocabulary of 210 words. It has been tested in second grade classes where it was read with ease.

Uses of This Book. Reading for fun. (And a little moral too.) Angela loves shoes and asks for nothing but shoes for her birthday. She gets what she wanted but finds out that sometimes you can get too much—even of a good thing.

Word List

All of the 210 words in *Shoes for Angela* are listed. Regular plurals (*-s*) and regular verb forms (*-s, -ed, -ing*) of words already on the list are not listed separately, but the endings are given in parentheses after the word.

5	Angela ('s)	I	wrote	all
	liked	need	to	the
	shoes	more	grandmother	aunts
	but	really	dear	uncle (s)
	had	do	you	cousins
	only	your	ask (ed)	can
	two	feet	what	use
	pair (s)	are	want	most
	one (s)	still	my	any
	was	grow (ing)	birthday	kind
	brown	her	would	love
	for	of	and	
	school	enough	size	**8** now
	black	**7** got	is	many
	good	an	2	dozens
6	said	idea	please	both
	mother	she	tell	big

small
when
they
new (s)
ran
out
buy
so
sensible
9 a
fine
little
girl (s)
10 who
money
11 course
12 on
mail
truck
stop (ped)
at
house
mailman
came
up
walk (ed)
with
pile
box (es)
higher
than
his
head
13 open (ed)
then
laugh (ed)

14 in
each
there
were
white
red
green
black
pink
blue
15 wear
skirt
straps
without
dancing
16 boots
rode
pony
shiny
church
high
snow
short
yellow
rain
17 young
sent
flippers
pool
just
right
18 every
pocket
bag
under
bed

dresser
closet
shelf
floor
19 so
that
quite
careless
once
living
room
sometimes
left
kitchen
or
steps
20 forgot
yard
fell
night
morning
full
water
21 look (ed)
terrible
oh
here
everywhere
22 fun
them
lot
work
change
play
riding

23 cleaned
shined
mess
nothing
put
ouch
25 I'm
afraid
these
too
see
if
wasn't
go (ing)
cry
guess
we'll
have
store
today
26 bought
3
wore
home
27 will
we
PTA
take
did
28 hair
eyes
everybody
happy
29 next
says
hats

The Follett BEGINNING-TO-READ Books

Purpose of the Beginning-to-Read Books: To provide easy-to-read materials that will appeal to the interests of primary children. Careful attention is given to vocabulary load and sentence length, but the first criterion is interest to children.

Reading Levels: These books are written at three reading levels, indicated by one, two, or three dots beneath the *Beginning-to-Read* symbol on the back cover. *Level One* books can be read by first grade children in the last half of the school year. As children increase their reading ability they will be able to enjoy *Level Two* books. And as they grow further in their reading ability they will progress to *Level Three* books. Some first grade children will read *Level Two* and *Level Three* books. Many third graders, and even some fourth graders, will read and enjoy *Level One* and *Level Two* books, as well as *Level Three* books. The range of interest of *Beginning-to-Read* books stretches far beyond their reading level.

Use of the Beginning-to-Read Books: Because of their high interest and readability, these books are ideal for independent reading by primary children—at school, in the library, and at home. The books may also be incorporated into the basic reading program to develop children's interests, expand their vocabularies, and improve word-attack skills. It has been suggested that they might serve as the foundation for a skillfully directed reading program. Many *Beginning-to-Read* books correlate with the social studies, science, and other subject fields. All will help children grow in the language arts. Children will read the *Beginning-to-Read* books with confidence, with success, and with real enjoyment.

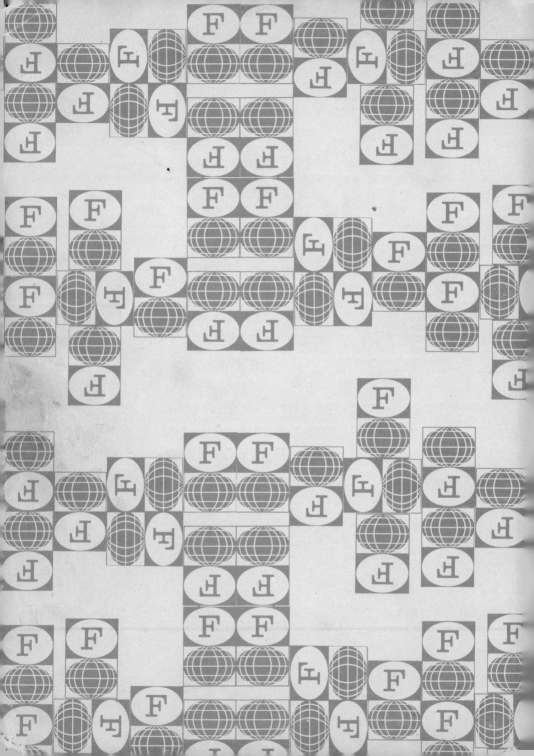